The Salt and Pepper Boys

RED FOX READ ALONE

It takes a special book to be a RED FOX READ ALONE!

If you enjoy this book, why not choose another READ ALONE from the list?

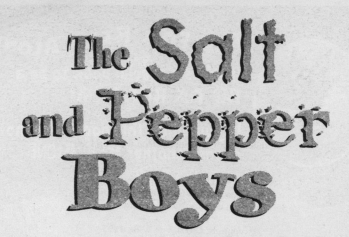

The Salt and Pepper Boys

JEAN WILLS

illustrated by Susan Varley

RED FOX

A Red Fox Book

Published by The Random House Group Ltd
20 Vauxhall Bridge Road, London, SW1V 2SA

A division of The Random House Group Ltd
London Melbourne Sydney Auckland
Johannesburg and agencies throughout the world

3 5 7 9 10 8 6 4 2

First published by Andersen Press Ltd 1993

Red Fox edition 1995

This Red Fox edition 1999

Printed and bound in Great Britain by
Cox & Wyman, Reading, Berkshire

RANDOM HOUSE UK Limited Reg. No. 954009

www.randomhouse.co.uk

ISBN 0 09 940142 8

Contents

To Uncle Charlie

1
Seaview Ghost House

Michael's mother peered out of the taxi.
VACANCIES said the notice in the
window.

'Stop, please,' she told the driver.
'I'll try here.'

The taxi drew up.

'Out you get.' His mother gave
Michael a push. 'And do try and look
cheerful.'

He didn't *feel* cheerful. They were
always moving on. Then his eyes
widened. The name on the gate
read . . . SEAVIEW GHOST
HOUSE.

Michael watched his mother on the
porch, sniffing the air. Cabbage,
drains, or boiled fish, and on they'd go.
Next door perhaps. To the LOBSTER
POTS PRIVATE HOTEL.

A boy ran out of the Seaview Ghost
House and looked at the gate.

'I knew Uncle Charlie had been up
to something!'

From inside a voice called, '*Len* . . .
NY!'

'No peace for the wicked,' said the boy.

Michael's mother had disappeared,
but inside the house she seemed to be
going loudly, *incredibly, MAD!* Then
she came out again, waving to the
driver to bring in the suitcases. Michael
followed. And so did Lenny.

'Who's *she?*'

'My mother,' Michael said.

'I mean, who *is* she?'

'Lorna Valetta, the singer.'

'Oh, a theatrical. They're all crazy.'

'Michael!' His mother beckoned.
'I've found an old friend. Come and
meet your Auntie Lily.'

A woman in an apron stepped
forward to hug Michael.

'*Swipe me!*' Lenny said.

Michael's mother hugged him too.

'I knew your mother once, years ago.'

Auntie Lily nodded. 'When me and my brother, Charlie, were kids.' She turned to Michael's mother. 'Charlie's an ice-cream man now.'

'No!'

'True as I'm standing here. While you pay the driver, I'll make a pot of tea. Just time for a chat before I start on the suppers.'

Lenny pulled at Michael's arm. A STOP ME AND BUY ONE man stood at the gate.

'Hello, Lenny boy. Who's this?'

'Michael Valetta. His mum's a theatrical. She knows you, Uncle Charlie.'

Uncle Charlie's eyebrows rose in the air like soaring eagles, but Lenny was pointing to the name on the gate.

'There were these letters, lying in the gutter. I couldn't resist it. Your mum angry?'

'No. But she will be.'

'I'll fix it, before she sees. Nip down the beach and tell Snaky Johnson I'll take all his lobsters.'

'If you'll give us two water-ices.'

Uncle Charlie opened his ice-box. He handed over the ices, and went into the house. *'Well, I'm bothered!'* they heard him say, and the madness began, all over again.

'Let's get out of it,' Lenny said.

Sucking their ices, they strolled down to the sea front. Lenny pointed out a fisherman, hauling his boat up the beach.

'That's Snaky Johnson.'

Moving closer, Michael saw two blue snakes tattooed on the fisherman's brown arms.

'Charlie wants all your lobsters,' called Lenny.

Snaky nodded, still hauling. His muscles rippled, and so did the snakes.

'Why does your uncle want so many lobsters?' Michael asked.

'To sell round the hotels and guest houses.'

They walked up the steps of the sea wall, and into the Municipal Gardens.

'Watch this.'

Lenny threw himself backwards, flipping over in the air. Landing on his feet. Just.

'Uncle Charlie showed me that. Shall I teach you?'

'No thanks.'

'Suit yourself.'

Lenny did another back flip, and landed in a flowerbed. A gardener chased them, and they hid behind the bandstand.

'Coming to school next week?' Lenny asked.

'I don't go to school. My mother teaches me.'

'You're kidding,' Lenny said.

Michael shook his head.

'Where?'

'Dressing-rooms, mostly. Between

rehearsals. Reading, writing, drawing, and singing. She's not much good at anything else.'

'What about arithmetic?'

'Glenda's better at that.'

'Who's Glenda?'

'The wardrobe lady.'

They left the gardens and walked past the grand hotels on the main promenade. Opposite the pier was the grandest building of all. The THEATRE ROYAL. They looked at the photographs outside. Lenny found Michael's mother.

'Not having to go to school!' Lenny still couldn't get over it.

High heels clicked down the theatre steps behind them. They saw seven pairs of legs and floral dresses.

Lenny pointed to the photographs.

'The *Floradora Dancers*. I saw them check in at the Lobster Pots.'

Michael looked across at the pier, stretching away into the sea.

'Got any money?' Lenny asked.

'I might have,' Michael said cautiously.

On the pier was THE TREASURE

CHEST, a glass case with a big metal claw inside. The *treasure* lay on the bottom. Michael put a penny in the slot.

'Try for that water pistol,' Lenny said. 'It's a good 'un.'

Michael moved the handle which worked the claw. It was nicely over the target when Lenny jogged him. The claw dipped and picked up . . .

'A shell necklace!' Lenny watched it slither down the chute. 'Who's a pretty boy then?'

Michael wanted to throw it in the sea, but Lenny stopped him.

'It might come in useful. Give it to me. Got another penny? Pay you back tomorrow. I get my job money Sundays.'

As the claw unfolded, he dived it at the water pistol.

'*Got it!*'

But it dropped to the bottom again.

They walked on. Michael saw sea
through the cracks in the floorboards.
He couldn't swim. And the end of the
pier still seemed miles away. When
they reached it at last, Lenny climbed
up behind a telescope.

'Got a threepenny?'

Michael found one and put it in the slot. The telescope swung free. They took turns looking at the fishing boats.

'My dad's a sailor,' Lenny said.

'Can you see his boat?'

'Not likely.' Lenny laughed. 'He's somewhere in the Pacific Ocean. Where's yours?'

'Paris.'

'Gone for long?'

'Gone for good.'

The threepenny ran out.

'I must be off an' all.'

Michael looked down at the waves splashing up the legs of the pier. It was always the same with people. There one minute, gone the next.

But Lenny was still standing there.

'If you're coming with me, you'll have to get a move on.'

2

Salt, Mustard, Vinegar, Pepper

Lenny glanced at the clock at the top of the pier.

'It's after five. I'll get my wages docked.'

'What is . . . your job?' Michael puffed as he kept up with Lenny.

'*Salt, mustard, vinegar, pepper.*'

What did he mean? Michael had no breath left to ask.

They turned off the promenade. Lenny stopped short at the gate of the . . . LOBSTER POOH PRIVATE HOTEL.

'I'll kill Uncle Charlie!'

As he ran into the Seaview Guest House, Auntie Lily appeared.

'The tables aren't done. You'll have me out of business. Guests won't stay if the meals aren't on time.'

'Don't fuss, Mum. I've got help.'

Lenny dragged Michael into the kitchen to wash his hands at the sink.

'Dining room next.'

He pointed to a row of salt and
pepper pots on a wooden trolley.

'Shake 'em first, to check, see? Any
empties, take to the kitchen for filling.
One set for each table.'

There were eight tables, but only
four were set with mats, knives, forks
and spoons.

'Next, mustard and vinegar. Check
the mustard spoons aren't mucky. And
don't spill vinegar on the cloths, or
Mum will serve you up in a pie. Bottles
of sauce stay on the trolley. Guests have
to ask for them. Serviettes. Different
coloured rings for each table . . .'

They just finished in time.

Michael sat at one of the tables with his mother and ate ham salad and boiled potatoes. She looked in surprise at his empty plate. He usually finished last.

Auntie Lily flew in with a red face and a treacle tart.

'You could do with some help,' Michael's mother told her.

'My sister's girls will be here soon. They come every summer, school holiday time.'

Michael didn't see Lenny again until next morning at breakfast. Sunday smart, hair flattened, Lenny brought newspapers to the tables. He gave Michael a penny.

'Just been paid. Coming out?'

But Michael had to do lessons all morning. It was Sunday dinner Salt and Pepper time before they met again.

'Lessons on a Sunday!' Lenny dropped a mustard pot. A yellow splodge landed on his hand. Without thinking, he licked it up. 'Phew! Help! I'm on fire! Pour me a glass of water. Quick!'

Auntie Lily came in and found mustard on the carpet.

'Fetch me a cloth. I've a good mind to dock your wages.'

When she stood up Lenny said, 'Hold out your hands, and shut your eyes.'

'No more of your silly nonsense.'
'But it's not. Honest!'
Auntie Lily closed one suspicious eye
at a time. When Lenny dropped the
shell necklace into her empty hand,
both eyes sprang open again.
'Where did you get this?'

'Out the Treasure Chest, specially for you.'

'You and your flannel! Worse than your Uncle Charlie. Which reminds me, he's late with that ice-cream. I want it for the cherry pie. Go and find him, and tell him to hurry.'

'But I haven't finished the tables.'

'I will,' Michael said.

Auntie Lily returned to the kitchen. When she came back she looked around.

'Good boy. Now you can sound the gong.'

He gave it a good walloping. As the sound died away, doors opened. His mother was first.

'Somebody wanted to make sure they were heard.'

Michael nodded. 'Yes. It was me.'

Lenny arrived with the ice-cream. Uncle Charlie had been held up making the Lobster Pooh Hotel respectable again.

Warm sunshine poured in the windows, but Michael had to stay indoors after dinner and do more lessons. Next week his mother would be extra busy, with rehearsals and costume fittings. The show opened the week after that.

Days fell into a pattern. Mornings, theatre. Afternoons, back to the Seaview Guest House, to watch for Lenny coming home from school. Being a Salt and Pepper boy.

'Fair's fair,' Lenny said. 'I'll pay you sixpence a week out my wages.'

When the show started, Michael spent Saturdays with Lenny as well.

'Behave yourself now,' Michael's mother said. 'Don't make extra work for Auntie Lily.'

Usually they went down to the beach to watch for Snaky Johnson's boat coming in. Or tailed Uncle Charlie through the town. On Sundays Michael's mother took them out.

The weather hotted up. And so did the Seaview Guest House. Flies buzzed into the kitchen. Lenny buzzed them out again. He buzzed one on an apple pie and made a crater in the pastry.

The NO VACANCIES sign went up. The Lobster Pots next door was full as well. Then Lenny came home and buzzed his shoebag up the path.

'That's it. No more school.'

Auntie Lily smiled. 'Tomorrow April and May will be here.' She went back into the kitchen.

'What did she mean?' Michael asked Lenny. 'Tomorrow's the end of July.'

'April and May are my cousins.'

Next day Lenny and Michael had just started on the tables when a taxi pulled up outside. Out jumped two large girls. The driver, laden with suitcases, staggered after them up the path.

'Behind the curtain, quick!' said Lenny. 'Unless you want a fate worse than death.'

'What's that?'

'Being *kissed*.'

'They wouldn't kiss *me*.'

'Want to bet?'

'*Len* . . . *NY!* THEY'RE HERE!'

'*Don't even breathe!*' Lenny hissed.

The floor shook. Salt and pepper pots rattled. Giggles filled the air.

'WHERE ARE YOU, YOU HORRIBLE LITTLE BOY?'

A bit of fluff went up Michael's nose. He sneezed. The curtains were flung back. Lenny dived under a table, but Michael was caught.

'Michael Valetta,' came Lenny's
voice from under the table. 'He's a
guest, so you'd better leave him alone.'
'Come out and kiss us, then we will.'
Stiffly, Lenny crawled out. Stiffly, he
clenched his jaw, and closed his eyes.

Afterwards, still giggling, April and May thundered up the staircase. A door banged at the top of the house.

'Don't you dare laugh,' Lenny said.

'I wasn't going to.'

'Which is worse, I can never decide. School, or April and May in August.'

'You've got me this year,' said Michael.

Lenny looked at him thoughtfully.

'Yes I have, haven't I? How about me coming with you to the theatre next week?'

3
April and May in August

'I don't know.' Auntie Lily looked at Lenny doubtfully.

'It will be company for Michael,' his mother said.

'Mind you behave then,' Auntie Lily told Lenny. 'No horseplay.'

'What's that?'

Lenny charged out, sending guests' beach shoes, buckets and spades

flying. Sand shot all over the path, and a shrimping net captured a small girl.

'It wasn't my fault,' Lenny protested, as they hurried along the promenade. 'Guests and their mess!'

In front clicked the heels of the *Floradoras*, who'd sat too long over breakfast. They all bundled together through the stage door at the side of the theatre.

Michael's mother shared a dressing-room with Madame Sidoni, the mind-reader. Madame Sidoni was standing on her head, feet up the dressing-room wall. It helped her think. Michael turned round to warn Lenny, but he wasn't there.

He shot out of the next door along.

'How was I to know it was the dancers' dressing-room? Don't they have any lights in this place?' Lenny stared at Madame Sidoni. '*Swipe me!*'

39

Madame Sidoni stared back, upside-down.

Lenny smiled. 'I can do a back flip.'

'*No!*' said Michael.

But Lenny had flipped. Madame Sidoni flopped. The pair of them collapsed in a tangle.

The door opened and a voice said, 'Five minutes, Madame Sidoni.'

'But I thought she was an acrobat,' Lenny protested after she'd gone. 'If she's a mind-reader, she should have known to stay out the way.'

'It's us who are supposed to keep out of the way,' Michael said.

He took Lenny to see Glenda, the wardrobe lady, but she was adding up bills.

'Don't disturb me, boys.' She pointed to a bag of toffees. Michael took several, then turned to find himself face to face with the dormouse from the Mad Hatter's Tea Party.

'It's only me,' came a fluffy voice.

Michael and the dormouse sat in the circle, sucking toffees and flicking the papers into the darkness.

'Well?' said Auntie Lily later. 'What

did you think of the theatre?'

'So-so,' said Lenny.

'That's because you didn't behave,' May said.

April nodded. 'We overheard the *Floradoras* in the Lobster Pots' garden.'

'To get a chance like that,' said May. 'And throw it away!'

'All right then.' Lenny filled a pepperpot. 'You go, instead of us.'

'If only . . .' April sneezed. '. . . we could.'

'Ask my mother,' Michael said, when they'd all stopped sneezing.

A few days later it was arranged. April and May went to morning rehearsal, while Lenny and Michael did the shopping instead.

'We can leave the shopping lists and baskets,' Lenny said. 'Then come back later and pick them up.'

The tide was out. They ran across the wet sand, stopping to make sandcastles and play French cricket with children staying at Seaview. Local children were jumping and diving from the pier into the sea.

Lenny stripped off, and splashed in to join them. Michael stayed in the

shallows, watching. If only he could
swim!

They were late at the shops. And that
wasn't the worst of it. Lenny had left
the butcher's list with the greengrocer.
The greengrocer's with the grocer.
And the grocer's with the butcher. By
the time they arrived back at Seaview
it was very late indeed.

Uncle Charlie stuck up for them.
'We were young once.'
'You've never grown up.'
Uncle Charlie was in disgrace. Last
night he'd hidden two lobster claws in
April and May's bed. The girls' screams
had been heard on the sea front.

Auntie Lily tossed her head.

'At least I can rely on April and May.'

But when they came back from the
theatre, April and May were changed
girls.

From that day on, right through to the end of August, they thought of nothing else but dancing. In and out of the tables, they danced. Upstairs. Downstairs. Round the garden. *All over* the Municipal Gardens. Along the promenade. Down the pier. They begged to be allowed to go to more rehearsals. Every step the *Floradoras* danced, they danced too.

4
Home Sweet Home

'*Glug, gloog, GLOOSH!*'

Lenny was teaching Michael to swim.

'We'll stop now. Don't want to drown you, do we?'

They dressed and went up on the promenade.

'How's he coming along?' asked Uncle Charlie.

'Just did six strokes,' Lenny said proudly.

Michael didn't say that during the last three, one foot had been on the bottom.

Uncle Charlie brought out two chocices.

'Hands off.' Behind them stood the *Floradoras*. 'Here you are, girls.'

'Thanks, Charlie. Been to our show yet?' one of them asked.

Uncle Charlie's eyebrows did a nose dive.

The dancer brought out a ticket.

'How about Saturday night? It'll be your last chance.'

Uncle Charlie's eyebrows almost took off. The dancers laughed and clicked away.

'Some people have all the luck,'
Lenny said.

'It's my fatal charm.'

'Oh yes? How about charming us
with water-ices?'

'If you go and tell Snaky Johnson I've
good homes for a dozen crabs.'

Snaky Johnson was waiting for the
tide. As he mended his nets, the snakes
wriggled. Michael followed Lenny into
the boat, which was even smaller than

the cramped little dressing-room his
mother shared with Madame Sidoni.

Later on, doing the tables, Michael
thought of being at sea in Snaky's boat.
Oh help! He'd spilt the vinegar!

April and May had to change the
tablecloth. They only just finished
before it was gong time.

'My turn,' Lenny said.

It grew hotter and hotter. August was
going out in style. Michael's mother
barely spoke, saving her voice for the
show. But Auntie Lily sang as she
peeled the potatoes.

'It's the end of the season,' Lenny
said. 'Soon she'll be able to take a rest.'
He frowned at a pepperpot. 'School
again.'

And moving on, Michael thought.
He couldn't bear to say it.

After the supper things were washed
and dried, April said, 'Can we go now,
Auntie Lily?'

'Back by nine, then.'

Lenny sniffed.

'It's not fair. If they go out, why can't we?'

'You're only shrimps,' May laughed, and off they went.

'Anyway, I've a job for you,' Auntie Lily said.

'All we ever do is jobs,' Lenny grumbled. 'Salt and Pepper boys. Flipping errand boys. Do this, do that, boys.'

The job was watering the garden,
where Lenny's dad grew roses and
geraniums when he was home from the
sea. Afterwards Lenny and Michael
squirted each other. Until the water
went over the wall and squirted some
Lobster Pots guests as well.

'That's it!'

As Auntie Lily pointed to the stairs, Uncle Charlie arrived with a left-over crab.

'You can't send the poor little blighters to bed in this heat.'

'You just watch me.'

Tired as he was, Uncle Charlie persuaded her to let him take them to the Municipal Gardens.

The band was playing. Uncle Charlie sank into a deckchair. In the middle of 'The Blue Danube' he nodded off.

Lenny raised his eyebrows. They were
thin little sparrows compared with
Uncle Charlie's eagles, but Michael
knew what they meant.

Down at the Theatre Royal were
April and May, drawn like magnets.
Lenny and Michael dodged them and
stopped at the Treasure Chest, but the
water pistol still stayed glued to the
bottom.

By the time they reached the end of
the pier, the sun had sunk into the sea.

'What's that?' Lenny said.

Above the waves and distant music,
Michael heard . . .

'Voices calling for help!'

'Where are they?'

Michael rushed forward and put his last threepenny in the slot, and swung the telescope.

'It's a rowing boat with two girls on board.'

Two girls!

They ran back to the land. April and May had gone.

'*Swipe me!*' said Lenny.

Snaky Johnson was in the pub. When Lenny told him what they'd seen, he hurried outside. As they reached Snaky's boat, there was a shout.

'Seen Lenny?'

'Down here, Charlie.'

High and dry in Snaky's boat, Michael and Lenny watched Uncle Charlie wade in, push off and jump aboard. Snaky started the engine.

The rosy glow over the sea turned purple, the water black. Snaky Johnson switched on his spotlight. It was Michael, used to dark theatres, who saw them first.

'*There!*'

Snaky cut the motor.

'*Help . . . help . . .*'

'Hold on, April and May. We're coming.' Uncle Charlie gripped hold of both boys. 'You two, don't move a muscle.'

But as Snaky Johnson beamed his spotlight, Lenny jumped up.

'That's not our April. Nor our May.'

'*They're Floradoras!*' said Michael.

The girls were hauled aboard. They'd
borrowed a rowing boat without
asking, and lost an oar. With the other
they'd gone round in circles, drifting
out on the tide.

'If it wasn't for these lads, you could
have been *Dead Doras*,' said Uncle
Charlie.

Snaky Johnson tied up the rowing boat, and turned for the shore.

The girls sobbed. Apart from the fright, they should be on stage. The show couldn't start without them.

But it had. April and May, who knew the *Floradoras'* every step, had danced in their place.

'Where have you three jokers been?' asked Auntie Lily when the boys and Uncle Charlie arrived at last. 'And where are April and May?'

Uncle Charlie's eyebrows zoomed.
'It's a bit of a long story.'
On Saturday night Uncle Charlie
wasn't alone in the front row of the
circle at the Theatre Royal. April and
May, Michael, Lenny, Snaky Johnson
and Auntie Lily were all there too. The
butcher's wife was looking after the
Seaview Guest House.

April and May danced their feet in time with the *Floradoras*. Madame Sidoni read Uncle Charlie's mind. Auntie Lily cried while Michael's mother sang *Home Sweet Home*. And Lenny swallowed a lump of rock, and had to go under the seat to recover.

Next day April and May went home. The place seemed quiet without them, though there were still a few guests left to keep the Salt and Pepper boys busy.

'Pity you're going,' Lenny told Michael. 'It's my birthday next week.' He threw salt over his shoulder for luck.

'Luck?' said Michael. 'There's no such thing.'

His mother fetched the suitcases. 'Time to pack up, Michael.'

Instead he ran outside, down the path, through the gate, to the promenade, and along to the pier. One by one, he fed his pennies into the Treasure Chest until they were gone.

Uncle Charlie rode up, ringing his bell.

'Everyone's looking for you. Time you went home.'

'I don't have a home.' Michael thumped the Treasure Chest. 'And I can't get that water pistol for Lenny's birthday, either.'

Uncle Charlie's eyebrows flapped.

'Hold on. Your mother and Auntie Lily have been cooking things up between them. How would you like to stay here the winter? Go to school with

Lenny?'

Lenny came running.

'Well?' said Uncle Charlie.

Can you guess what Michael said?

SALLY GRINDLEY

Mulberry
out on the town

Illustrated by Tania Hurt-Newton

MACDONALD YOUNG BOOKS

Mulberry pulled on his lead.
"Faster," he barked, "faster."
"Slow down, Mulberry," they said.
But Mulberry was in a hurry to go
to the shops.

When they got to the first shop,
Mulberry stopped and sniffed. Delicious
meaty smells floated up his nose.
He tugged hard on his lead.

"No, Mulberry," they said.
"Dogs have to wait outside."
They tied his lead to a rail
and went inside.

Mulberry waited and waited, but nobody came. Then he saw another dog trotting along. She looked just like him.

Mulberry pulled on his lead and
tried to catch up with her.
"Don't go," he cried.

The other dog licked him on the nose
and trotted off.

Mulberry tugged and tugged at his
lead. Suddenly, it came loose.
"Wait for me," he barked and ran
after the other dog.

I'm coming
with you.

"Shoo," shouted her people.
Mulberry stopped. He didn't like cross
voices. His ears drooped and his tail
hung down.

On the way back, Mulberry stopped and sniffed. Delicious smells of bread floated up his nose. He followed the smells into a baker's shop.

Inside the door was a basket full of
rolls. Mulberry grabbed one in his
mouth. Someone shouted at him
and tried to grab his collar.
Mulberry ran away.

Mulberry couldn't see his people
anywhere.
"Where are you?" he howled.
He trotted into a shop. Fluffy things
stared at him. Mulberry stared back.

He grabbed a teddy by the foot, and
shook it and shook it and shook it.
"Stop it!" shouted a voice.
Mulberry didn't like cross voices.
He dropped the teddy and ran away.

Suddenly, Mulberry saw them. They
were upstairs. But he was downstairs.
They were going up some moving
stairs. He ran to the bottom.
"Stop!" he howled. "I want
to get on."
The stairs kept moving.

Wait for me!

Mulberry put his front paws on. But
then the stairs moved and he fell flat
on his tummy.

Now he was going up.
"Wait for me," he barked again.
But they were walking away. When he
reached the top, they had gone again.

Mulberry looked around and sniffed.
Delicious biscuity smells floated up
his nose.

In a shop there was a whole barrel full
of biscuits. He stood up on his back legs
and reached into the barrel. The barrel
fell over.

Crunchy things were everywhere.
Mulberry ate as many as he could.
Then he trotted off round the shop.

There was a cage on the floor.
Mulberry peered inside. Three pairs
of eyes stared back.

"I can see you," barked Mulberry.
He ran from side to side. The rabbits
ran from side to side as well.

"Stop it!" shouted a voice. "Out,
out, out!"
Mulberry didn't like cross voices.
He ran out of the shop, grabbing
some crunchy things on the way.

Now Mulberry was feeling tired. He went into another shop and looked around. There were beds in this shop, lots of them.

Mulberry found a bed right in the corner. He jumped up, made himself comfy, and closed his eyes. Soon he was fast asleep.

Mulberry was woken by a shout.
"What's that dog doing in my shop?"
He leapt to his feet. People were
standing all round the bed.

Mulberry howled with fright. He had
heard enough cross voices for one day.
And this voice was very cross!
Mulberry ran as fast as his legs would go.

Now Mulberry wanted to go home.
"Where are you?" he howled.
And then he saw them down below.
He ran to the top of the moving stairs.

He put a paw on the stairs and took it off again quickly.

"Come and get me," he howled, and at last they saw him.

"Stay, Mulberry, stay," they cried.
Mulberry didn't need to be told twice.
He stayed.

When they reached the top of the
stairs, he leapt up at them.
"I'm so pleased to see you," he barked.
"Can we go home now?"

They patted him on the head and took hold of his lead.

As they walked home, Mulberry sniffed.
Delicious meaty smells came from the
shopping bag. Mulberry sniffed it.
"Yes, it's for you," they laughed,
"when we get home."

Look out for more of Mulberry's adventures:

Mulberry Goes to School by Sally Grindley

Mulberry has sneaked into school. He has fun with a skipping-rope in the playground until someone wants to chase him. Then he meets the caretaker, who's not happy about Mulberry's mucky pawprints. And when Mulberry gets trapped in a cupboard, he decides he's learnt enough for one day.

Mulberry Alone at the Seaside by Sally Grindley

Mulberry has come to the seaside. He has great fun splashing in the sea and knocking down sand-castles. He even helps himself to someone's picnic. But when Mulberry is trapped by the tide, he decides he's had enough of the seaside for one day.

Mulberry Alone on the Farm by Sally Grindley

Mulberry visits a farm for the day. He runs off to look for someone to play with, but the hens, the piglets and the scarecrow don't want to play with him. Mulberry is fed up, until the sky grows dark and he gets caught in a scary thunderstorm.

All these books in the Mulberry series can be purchased from your local bookseller. For more information about Mulberry, write to: *The Sales Department, Hodder Headline, 338 Euston Road, London, NW1 3BH*